BIG RED BARN

Margaret Wise Brown

pictures by Felicia Bond

Harper & Row, Publishers

Text copyright 1956, © 1989 by Roberta Brown Rauch   Illustrations copyright © 1989 by Felicia Bond   Printed in the U.S.A.
1 2 3 4 5 6 7 8 9 10   All rights reserved.   Newly illustrated edition   Library of Congress Cataloging-in-Publication Data   Brown, Margaret Wise, 1910-1952.
Big red barn.   Summary: Rhymed text and illustrations introduce the many different animals that live in the big barn.
[1. Domestic animals—Fiction. 2. Farm life—Fiction. 3. Stories in rhyme] I. Bond, Felicia, ill. II. Title.
PZ8.3.B815Big 1989   [E]   85-45814   ISBN 0-06-020748-5   ISBN 0-06-020749-3 (lib. bdg.)
Text changes made with the permission of the Estate of Margaret Wise Brown

By the big red barn
In the great green field,

There was a pink pig
Who was learning to squeal.

There was a great big horse
And a very little horse.

And on every barn
Is a weather vane, of course—
A golden flying horse.

There was a big pile of hay
And a little pile of hay,
And that is where the children play.

But in this story the children are away.
Only the animals are here today.

The sheep and the donkey,
The geese and the goats,
Were making funny noises
Down in their throats.

An old scarecrow
Was leaning on his hoe.

And a field mouse was born

In a field of corn.

Cock-a-doodle-dooooo!
In the barn there was a rooster
And a pigeon, too.

And a big white hen
Standing on one leg.
And under the hen was a quiet egg.

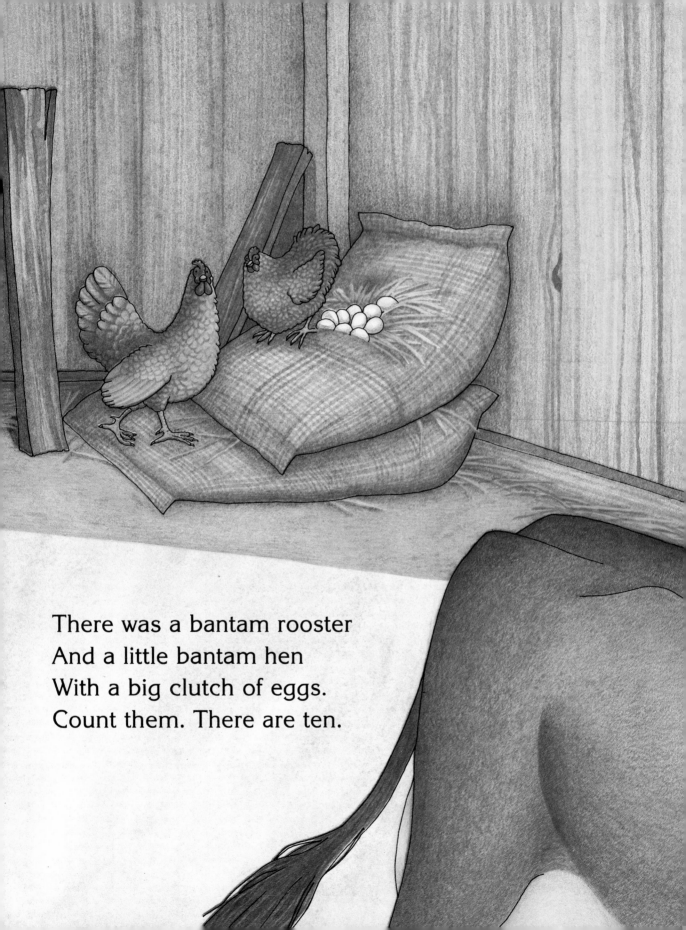

There was a bantam rooster
And a little bantam hen
With a big clutch of eggs.
Count them. There are ten.

Cock-a-doodle-doo!
Moooooooooo! Moo!
There was a big brown cow
And a little brown cow.

There was an old black cat,
Meow! Meow!
And a tiger tomcat,
Yeow! Yeow!

There was a big red dog,
Bow! Wow!
With some little puppy dogs
All round and warm.

And they all lived together
In the big red barn.

And they played all day
In the grass and in the hay.

When the sun went down
In the great green field,
The big cow lowed,
The little pig squealed.

The horses stomped in the sweet warm hay,
And the little donkey gave one last bray.

The hens were sleeping on their nests.
Even the roosters took a rest.
The little black bats flew away
Out of the barn at the end of the day.

And there they were all night long

Sound asleep

In the big red barn.

Only the mice were left to play,
Rustling and squeaking in the hay,

While the moon sailed high

In the dark night sky.

DATE DUE

2-11-91			
FEB 14 '91			
MAY 14 '91			
SEP 2 2 '91			
AUG 0 1 1991			
DEC. 4 1991			
FEB. 1 7 1992			
APR 2 8 1992			
OCT 2 8 1992			
DEC. 0 4 1993			
MAY 1 1 1994			
JUN 8 1995			
JUL 1 8 1995			
OCT 0 3 95			
APR 15 98			
SEP 12 2002 ILL# 9369136B GN②			
GAYLORD			PRINTED IN U.S.A.